TREV THE TUDOR
Gets the Chop (nearly)

SCOULAR ANDERSON

SCHOLASTIC

For Jennifer

Scholastic Children's Books,
Commonwealth House, 1-19 New Oxford Street,
London WC1A 1NU, UK

A division of Scholastic Ltd
London ~ New York ~ Toronto ~ Sydney ~ Auckland
Mexico City ~ New Delhi ~ Hong Kong

Published in the UK by Scholastic Ltd, 2001

ISBN 0 439 99254 0

Printed by Cox & Wyman Ltd, Reading, Berks

2 4 6 8 10 9 7 5 3 1

CONTENTS

WHO'S WHO

MY MUM

MY SISTER MEG

ME - TREVOR TWYNBARROW

SHE'S A GOOD LAUNDRESS

SHE'S AN EVEN BETTER LAUNDRESS

CLEM SWALLOW

COUSIN JOHN PARCHMYNT

MISTRESS PARCHMYNT

MY BEST MATE. LOOKING FOR A GAME OF FOOTBALL

...AND DREAMING OF OWNING A BLUE SILK SUIT

HE'S GOT A PRIVY * INSIDE HIS HOOSE!!

* TOILET

4

5

The Road to the Village

I had my breeches round my ankles and I was having a pee when I heard my mate Clem Swallow call me.

I was supposed to be looking after our pig Bessy. Bessy is the most valuable thing we have. But I really wanted to see Old Clapperdudgeon. My ma was busy so I tied Bessy to a tree. She'd be fine for a while.

We took a short cut through the wood. The charcoal burners were there. They burn wood in heaps that look like great pies. They stack the wood in a very special way.

They cover the wood with earth then they set it on fire.

The charcoal burners have to watch their great, smoking pies day and night. That's why they live in huts and tents in the middle of the woods. They're a bit strange.

I found a little bit of charcoal.

I don't know how Clem knows these things. Perhaps if I lived in the village instead of the middle of nowhere, I'd know things, too.

We took another short cut through an enclosure. These fences and hedges weren't here when I was a tot. Clem knows about them, too. He's a right know-all.

Clem says people are losing their jobs because of the sheep.

Well, now he mentioned it, yes, quite a few folk had been up to our cottage. Ma gave them some food or a coin – and *we're* not rich. I wondered if we might be thrown out of our house, too.

We came down into the village. There was a lot going on. Old Clapperdudgeon looked fairly cheerful. Someone had brought him a jar of ale from Widow Waynscote's.

Old Clapperdudgeon was there because he had been making a nuisance of himself. As he is an old man he is allowed to beg.
He is always showing us
his official certificate.

When he's in a good mood, Old Clapperdudgeon shows us his ear which has a hole right through it.

Sometimes, when he's in a really good mood, he'll show us his back.

Widow Waynscote came bustling past.

Old Clapperdudgeon took out his whistle and played a tune or two.

Some other people had arrived at the village. They were a funny looking lot.

Old Clapperdudgeon called out to them.

The Egyptians are travelling folk. They're sometimes called Gyptians or Gypsies. Their dancing was great.

OUR VILLAGE of SHEEPWASHE

① OLD CLAPPERDUDGEON IN THE STOCKS AS A PUNISHMENT FOR BEING A NUISANCE. SOMETIMES WE COME TO THROW THINGS AT HIM.

② WIDOW WAYNSCOTE'S PLACE. SHE BREWS BEER TO SELL.
③ WALTER WALTHEW'S HOUSE. HE'S A

WOOLDRIVER WHO HAS A FLEET OF MULES TO CARRY WOOL TO AND FROM MARKET.

16

④ FARMER FLASKE'S BIG HOUSE.

⑤ HIS GRAINSTORE ON STILTS TO KEEP OUT RATS.

⑥ MR SWARTE THE MILLER AND HIS MILL.

⑦ WILL THE WARRENER WHO LOOKS AFTER FARMER FLASKE'S RABBIT WARREN. HE'S OFF TO MARKET TO SELL SOME RABBITS.

⑧ WIDOW TWYNE'S HOUSE. SHE'S A WISE WOMAN WHO GROWS HERBS FOR HEALING. CLEM SAYS SHE'S CALLED A WITCH BUT SHE SEEMS A KIND OLD LADY.

Someone else came into the village just after the dancing. It was the swigman. Everyone likes to see the swigman or pedlar. He sells all sorts of exciting things. (Clem reckons he steals half of them.)

He opened his packs and boxes and we all crowded round.

There are no shops in the village so everyone was desperate to buy something. The swigman might not pass again for many weeks.

POTS, PINS AND IRONING STICKS...

... SCARVES, NAPKINS AND LACE...

...BEADS, BANGLES AND RINGS...

... PERFUME, GLOVES AND STOCKINGS...

...TOYS, PAPER AND INK...

...AND FOR THOSE WHO COULD READ — RUDE SONGS AND POEMS.

The swigman brought another thing which everyone wanted – gossip and news from elsewhere.

The swigman's news always keeps people gossiping for ages. As the swigman went off for a jar of ale, something else happened in the village...

FOOTBALL!

The lads from the next village had come to challenge us. The younger Gyptians said they would join our side. The ball was placed on the path, halfway between the two villages. If we got the ball back to our own village, we won.

Football is always a wild game.

We won but the villagers weren't pleased. They're never pleased when the football starts.

Clem and I made a quick
exit. We took a short
cut over Gallows Hill.
I had never been to
Gallows Hill. I
didn't ever want
to go back!

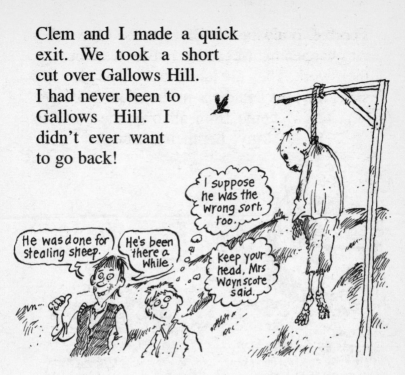

I hurried on home. I had the feeling I was in for
trouble after being away so long.

23

I peered round the side of the house to see what was happening. Ma and my sister were busy at their work. They are laundresses. They say my sis is the best laundress in the country. People come from all over the place to give her their washing.

MA WASHING CLOTHES. SHE USES GOOEY SOAP MADE FROM FAT AND ASH.

WASHING LAID OUT ON THE GRASS TO DRY.

SIS SETTING THE BUCK. IT'S A HUGE TUB. CLOTHES ARE LAID IN THERE IN A VERY SPECIAL WAY — SEPARATED BY STICKS — SO THAT WATER WILL FLOW THROUGH EASILY. STUFF CALLED LYE (THAT'S WATER MIXED WITH ASHES) IS POURED THROUGH TO CLEAN THE CLOTHES.

THE BLEACHING BUCKET WHERE WASHING IS LEFT TO BLEACH WHITE. PEE IS THE BEST THING FOR BLEACHING SO WE KEEP A SPECIAL POT FOR IT...

...oops! I was in the middle of filling the special pot when Clem came!

Ma had spotted me...

I lay in bed and tried not to think of the smell of the bread Ma was baking. I thought about the things I had never seen, like shops and ships.

I didn't know that I was going to visit the town sooner than I thought.

27

The Road to the Town

The next day there was a large cart waiting to take us to the town. It seemed we were to be turned out of our house after all. Luckily, we had somewhere else to stay. John Parchmynt is a rich merchant and a cousin of my dead dad. My mum and sis were going to work for him so we would be living in his big house. We were going to be RICH!

It so happened that my mate Clem was also moving to the town. He was going to become an apprentice.

He showed me his contract. It meant nothing to me so he had to read it out loud.

Contract of Apprenticeship to Mr Joshua Meager, Master Tailor of Great Figton, with Clement Swallow. During his apprenticeship he shall not play dice or cards or get drunk. He shall not take up unhonest company. He shall not marry neither shall he dally with any of his master's maidservants. He will be supplied with meat, drink and linen, woollen garments, stockings, shoes and bedding.

Joshua Meager. Tailor

The road to the town was bigger than I thought. It was busy and muddy. The carter pointed things out to us along the way.

31

When we got to Cousin Parchmynt's house I was amazed how big it was.

GREAT FIGTON

THE CROWN INN

① WE COULD HAVE BROUGHT BESSIE INSTEAD OF SELLING HER — PEOPLE IN TOWN HAVE PIGS, TOO.

② OLD CLAPPERDUDGEON WOULD BE AT HOME HERE. THEY'VE GOT A NICE NEW PILLORY.

③ THE TOWN COUNCILLORS ARE GOING UP INTO THEIR COUNCIL ROOM ABOVE THE MARKET HALL.

④ THEY'RE PROBABLY GOING TO DECIDE WHAT TO DO WITH THE TWO LADS IN THE CAGE BELOW THE STAIRS.

— THEY'VE BEEN MISBEHAVING. THEY'RE THE WRONG SORT. YOU WON'T CATCH ME IN THERE. I'M KEEPING MY HEAD.

⑤ THE PUBLIC WEIGHING PLACE WHERE PEOPLE GET THINGS WEIGHED.

Cousin Parchmynt is very proud of his house.

He showed us round. It was amazing. The walls in the hall are covered in wooden panels.

The windows have glass in them so you can see out but the weather can't get in.

On the sideboard, all the plates and cups were on display.

The furniture is carved. There are comfy cushions on the chairs.

The beds are enormous.

OF COURSE, MY BED ISN'T AS GRAND AS THIS. I SLEEP ON A TRUCKLE-BED – THAT'S A LITTLE BED ON WHEELS WHICH IS KEPT UNDER THE BIG BED.

There is even a privy – INDOORS!

I was just about to ask Cousin Parchmynt a question...

...when my ma dragged me off to have a bath. Then I was given some new clothes and some shoes. I had never worn shoes before. They were really strange.

It was time for dinner. I had never seen food like it. Cousin Parchmynt is very proud of his food.

The servants all came in and stood and Cousin Parchmynt said a little prayer, then we all tucked in.

At the end of the meal there were more surprises which I had never seen or tasted.

After dinner, Cousin Parchmynt took me into the parlour. He put some stuff called tobacco into a pipe, then lit it. He said it was very fashionable.

Cousin Parchmynt gave me a little talk.

So, the very next day, I was sent to Mr Cribtree's school.

Any mischief and it's the BIRCH!

There were 20 other boys in the school and it was very noisy. At school I learned to read.

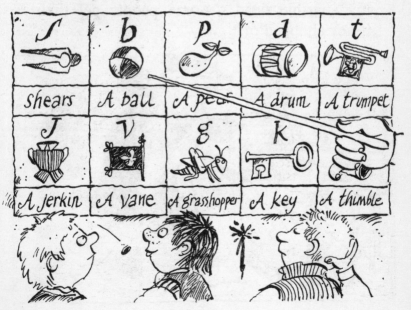

Shears · A ball · A pear · A drum · A trumpet · A jerkin · A vane · A grasshopper · A key · A thimble

I learned to
write and do
sums.

I learned to
sing.

I only got the birch twice. At least I still had
my sensible head – some people get their
heads chopped off!

But it seemed to me that Clem was getting ahead quicker than me. Mr Meager, the tailor, had given Clem some new clothes.

Clem told me there are laws which tell you which clothes you can wear and which ones you can't.

As Mr Meager was out on business, Clem took me into the shop and showed me how a rich man dresses.

① CLEM SLEEPS UNDER THE COUNTER.

② HE HAS TO CLEAN THE SHOP EACH DAY.

③ CLEM PUTS ON A LONG SHIRT FIRST.

④ CLEM PULLS ON BREECHES THAT STRETCH TO THE KNEE.

⑤ THE CODPIECE IS TIED UP WITH LACES—HANDY WHEN YOU WANT TO FILL A BLEACH POT!

Just as Clem had finished dressing there was a shout from an apprentice outside.

When the apprentices heard that they left their work and came out into the street for a bit of fun. The apprentices from one end of town chased those from the other end. The girls came out to watch, but the shopkeepers were furious.

It was a bit like football without the ball, really. Cousin Parchmynt came to drag me away. He was really annoyed I had got so dirty. He told me my sis was far more sensible. It seems she's getting ahead without having to go to school.

Your sister is going to work for the Countess of Drybale at Drybale Hall.

It is a great honour for me that the Countess has asked for my laundry-maid.

After my sis had been working for the Countess for a month, Cousin Parchmynt took me to see her at Drybale Hall. We went by horse but, you know, I don't think Cousin was very good at using a horse.

My sis is a very important person now. She is chief laundry maid and has three maids and one porter working under her.

Not only is she in charge of cleaning the linen, she also looks after the Countess's clothes.

① SIS LET ME TRY ON THE STARCHED CUFFS AND RUFFS RICH PEOPE WEAR. HOW DO THEY DO ANYTHING?

② FUR-TRIMMED CLOTHES HAVE TO BE BRUSHED ONCE A WEEK TO KEEP THE MOTHS AWAY.

③ ALL SORTS OF HERBS ARE USED TO REMOVE STAINS.

④ ONE OF THE COUNTESS'S CORSETS (STUFFED WITH REEDS!)

⑤ HER FARTHINGALE —A THING MADE OF WILLOW CANES TO MAKE HER DRESSES STICK OUT NICELY!

I was told to go out into the garden while Cousin spoke to the Countess. A little later I had to go and sing for the Countess.

① THE COUNTESS'S HOME - DRYBALE HALL.

② THERE'S A LONG GALLERY THAT STRETCHES THE LENGTH OF THE HOUSE. PEOPLE WALK UP AND DOWN AND CHAT TO EACH OTHER HERE.

③ JOKE FOUNTAIN THAT SURPRISES PEOPLE BY SQUIRTING WATER AS THEY PASS BY. BRILLIANT!

She was very impressed. She also liked the drawing I had done of her house on the back of my music sheet. I used the bit of charcoal I had picked up in the woods back home.

④ DOVECOT FOR PIGEONS — ROAST PIGEON AND EGGS FOR DINNER!

⑤ DR HALFPENNY AND DR FOXWELL DISCUSSING TWO NEW PLANTS WHICH HAVE JUST BEEN BROUGHT FROM SOUTH AMERICA. DR HALFPENNY IS GOING TO EAT THEIR FRUIT. DR FOXWELL SAYS HE'LL DROP DEAD. THEY'RE CALLED POTATO AND TOMATO.

The Road to the City

A few days later, Cousin Parchmynt was in a very excited mood.

Cousin Parchmynt told me that meant I was her personal servant and messenger.

I had to go to London – WOW! The Countess was moving to her London house because she was going to visit the Queen at court. Just about everything but the kitchen sink came with us.

...10 hat-boxes, 15 chests of linen, 12 chests of dresses, the great bed from the west chamber...

At last we were off. My sis came too, as she would be needed in London.

Saying goodbye to Mum was quite tearful.

London is a huge place. We went through one of the gates in the city wall. There was a haze in the sky from the thousands of smoking chimneys.

① ONE OF THE GATES IN THE CITY WALL.

② THE GATEKEEPER SPAT OUT OF THE WINDOW AND HIT OUR CART-DRIVER IN THE EYE.

③ THERE ARE SO MANY PEOPLE IN LONDON THAT THE HOUSES SPILL OUT ONTO LAND BEYOND THE WALL.

④ THERE'S A CHURCH ROUND EVERY CORNER! THE BIG ONE IS ST PAUL'S CATHEDRAL. IT'S LOST ITS SPIRE.

⑤ A COOK-HOUSE WHERE PEOPLE WITHOUT KITCHENS HAVE THEIR FOOD COOKED — OR COME FOR TAKE-AWAYS.

⑥ THEY DEFINITELY LOOK THE WRONG SORT.

Once we were through the gate, I jumped down from the cart so I could see what was going on. The wide streets were crammed with people. The smaller streets were too narrow for carts. This was far more exciting than the village or the town even!

Once we had arrived at the Countess's city house, I had to dress up in her livery – the suit of clothes all her servants wear. (Blue silk, Clem!)

That evening there was a feast at the palace. The Countess told her nephew, Sir Sydney Spanyell, to keep an eye on me.

Always bow when someone looks in your direction.

Thank goodness I've got in with the right sort at last!

① THE PALACE IS LIKE THE RABBIT WARREN BACK IN SHEEPWASHE– SO MANY DOORS AND ROOMS AND CORRIDORS!

② SIR SYDNEY ALWAYS CARRIES A POMANDER FULL OF SWEET HERBS–IT KEEPS AWAY NASTY SMELLS.

The palace was full of people in fabulous clothes. They all pretended not to look at each other while they hoped that everyone was looking at them. Posers, in other words.

There was definitely plenty of gossip going on.

At the feast, I had to stand behind the Countess's chair. She was furious that she had been seated 173 places away from the Queen. Perhaps she doesn't know the Right Sort of people?

All the plates, cups and cutlery were made of silver and my mouth watered when I saw the delicious food.

IT WAS AMAZING - FAR BETTER THAN COUSIN PARCHMYNT'S. THE BEST THING WAS A GIANT PIE IN THE SHAPE OF A CASTLE.

BLAH!

EACH COURSE WAS ANNOUNCED BY A FANFARE OF TRUMPETS

AFTER THE MAIN MEAL, SPECIAL GUESTS WERE INVITED TO THE BANQUETING ROOM TO EAT SWEETS

PEARS IN SYRUP

WAFERS, CUPS AND PLATES ALL MADE OF SUGAR!

CUBES OF JELLY

When all the guests had gone, the servants fought for the left-overs. I was starving!

Sir Sydney Spanyell asked me to go and find a piss-pot for him. Cousin Parchmynt might have an indoor privy, but there aren't many in the palace!

The rest of the evening was spent in dancing and watching a masque, which is a sort of musical entertainment.

I was asked to sing for the Queen! She smiled and said I had an excellent voice. Afterwards, Sir Sydney said:

I told him I was keeping my head and he sneered.

After the visit to the palace I spent most of the time running errands for Sir Sydney Spanyell. I'd never met anyone who sent so many letters.

I got to know London pretty well. Cousin Parchmynt would have been proud of me. I had got to know lots of people and I'm sure they were all the Right Sort.

① THERE ARE ONLY A FEW BROAD STREETS IN THE CITY THAT CARTS OR PEOPLE ON HORSEBACK CAN USE. THE REST ARE VERY NARROW.
② MOSTLY THEY ARE VERY SMELLY BECAUSE OF ALL THE MUCK HEAPS.

Saint Paul's Cathedral is enormous. It is a busy place inside because people use it as a street. They walk in one door and out the other. They hold business meetings in the middle of it.

If you're searching for a job, you look at the notices pinned on the Cathedral doors.

You have to watch your valuables – the Cathedral is a favourite haunt for thieves.

I overheard all sorts of interesting gossip in Saint Paul's.

I found the man with the white flower in his hat. I handed over my letter and hurried back home.

When I was sent to deliver another letter next day, there was a fair in one of the broad streets.

There were musicians and dancers.

There were puppets
and side-shows.

There were dancing bears and counting dogs.

There were wrestling matches and weight-lifting competitions.

Sir Sydney was furious that I took so long to return, but there was so much to see at the fair. He told me that the next day I had to go on a very difficult errand. I was to cross the river to the theatres. I was so excited I couldn't sleep. I even heard the night watchman go past in the street below.

The Road to the World

The following day, Sir Sydney gave me another letter.

You must give this to an actor. He'll be wearing an ass's head.

I had to make my way to the River Thames.

① IT'S USUALLY QUICKER TO TRAVEL BY WATER BECAUSE THE STREETS ARE SO NARROW AND BUSY.

THERE ARE ABOOUT TWO THOUSAND FERRYMEN!

② THE FERRYMEN CRY OUT EITHER 'WESTWARD-HO!' OR 'EASTWARD HO!' DEPENDING ON WHICH WAY THEY WANT TO GO.

③ THE FERRYMEN GRUMBLE A LOT BECAUSE THEIR FARES HAVE BEEN FIXED AT THE SAME PRICE FOR YEARS.

④ THE QUEEN OFTEN TRAVELS BY BARGE— THREE ROYAL PALACES SIT BY THE RIVER.

⑤ A HUGE WATER-TOWER. WATER IS PUMPED UP TO THE TOP THEN IT FLOWS THROUGH PIPES TO IMPORTANT HOUSES.

① I MET THIS OLD FELLOW WHO STARTED TO TELL ME THINGS ABOUT THE BRIDGE.

② HE SAID THAT SOMETIMES THE HEADS ARE HALF-BOILED AND COATED IN TAR TO KEEP THEM IN SHAPE.

③ THERE ARE NINETEEN ARCHES. (I DIDN'T COUNT.)

There is only one bridge across the River Thames – London Bridge. It is quite a size! There are hundreds of houses on it and shops as well. The heads of people who have been executed are stuck on poles on top of the entrance. They lost their heads because they were a danger to the Queen. The ravens and kites were having a fine picnic!

④ WHEN THE TIDE IS LOW THERE IS QUITE A DROP IN LEVEL BETWEEN WATER ABOVE AND BELOW THE BRIDGE... SO.. ⑤ YOUNG FOOLS SHOW OFF (HIS WORDS) BY 'SHOOTING THE BRIDGE' IN BOATS AND OFTEN DROWN THEMSELVES.

At the start of the bridge there's a big water wheel that pumps water from the river to people's houses.

The bridge is busy. You really have to squeeze yourself against the wall when a cart comes by.

On the other side I had to find the right theatre.

The first place I went into wasn't the right one. It certainly wasn't a play that was being performed.

I came out again quickly.

I got it right the second time. A flag was flying above the theatre, which meant a play was about to start. Crowds of people were heading for the theatre. There were all sorts – rich people as well as shopkeepers and apprentices.

THIS IS AN EVEN BETTER PLACE THAN ST PAUL'S FOR THIEVES! I KNOW ALL ABOUT THIEVING NOW. I WON'T TRY MYSELF AS I'M GETTING AHEAD. I WATCHED A YOUNG THIEF CUT SOMEONE'S PURSE.

BUT THERE WAS ONLY ONE COIN IN IT!

Curses!

I SAW ANOTHER THIEF CUT A REALLY FAT PURSE.

Pies! Hot pies!

THEN HE TUGGED AT HIS MATE'S CLOAK AS A SIGN FOR HER TO TAKE THE PURSE.

BUT HE TUGGED THE WRONG CLOAK! THE YOUNG THIEF COULDN'T BELIEVE HIS LUCK.

HE TOOK THE PURSE THEN TUGGED THE CLOAK OF THE OTHER THIEF'S MATE...

...AND HANDED HER THE EMPTY PURSE HE HAD JUST STOLEN. THEN HE MOVED AWAY.

You're useless, Tom Tyte!

79

1. THIS IS THE ACTOR WITH THE ASS'S HEAD WHO'S TO GET MY LETTER.

2. THE ACTORS ARE WEARING REALLY FANCY COSTUMES.

3. WOMEN AREN'T ALLOWED TO ACT SO THE WOMEN'S PARTS ARE PLAYED BY BOYS. I SUPPOSE I COULD TRY ACTING TO GET AHEAD — AN ASS'S HEAD! HO-HO!

The theatre was absolutely brilliant!

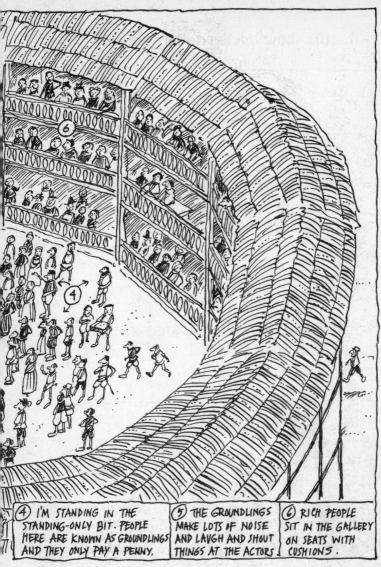

④ I'M STANDING IN THE STANDING-ONLY BIT. PEOPLE HERE ARE KNOWN AS GROUNDLINGS AND THEY ONLY PAY A PENNY.

⑤ THE GROUNDLINGS MAKE LOTS OF NOISE AND LAUGH AND SHOUT THINGS AT THE ACTORS.

⑥ RICH PEOPLE SIT IN THE GALLERY ON SEATS WITH CUSHIONS.

I watched a whole play called 'A Midsummer Night's Dream' by a Mr Shakespeare.

After the show I delivered my letter.

I had just crossed the bridge again when I heard a familiar voice call me – it was my old mate Clem Swallow!

It turned out he had joined the crew of a ship that was going on a voyage of exploration. He had got fed up being an apprentice tailor and run away. Now Clem wanted to be far away before Mr Meager caught up with him. He showed me round the ship.

Below deck it was dark and smelly. Clem showed me where he slept.

He showed me where the privy was. It's called the Heads and it's right at the front of the ship. I suppose there isn't much point in having a piss-pot for bleach there!

He introduced me to Slush the cook. The menu didn't look very interesting.

① SHIP'S BISCUITS (INSTEAD OF BREAD)— YOU HAD TO TAP THEM FIRST TO KNOCK OUT THE WEEVILS AND MAGGOTS.

③ BULLY BEEF— THAT WAS BOILED BEEF. THE BEEF HAD BEEN PACKED IN BARRELS WITH SALT TO PRESERVE IT.

④ SEA PIE—LAYERS OF MEAT SEPARATED BY SHIP'S BISCUITS— PLUS A MAGGOT OR TWO.

⑤ SALAMAGUNDY— SLICES OF SALT FISH AND ONIONS BOILED AND BOILED.

⑥ DRIED PEAS— MR SLUSH MADE THEM INTO PORRIDGE— OR SOUP (DEPENDING ON HOW MUCH WATER HE ADDED).

② BEER AND WATER. ON A LONG VOYAGE THEY BOTH SOON GET SLIMY AND STALE.

⑦ LOBSCOUSE— SALT MEAT, SHIP'S BISCUITS AND ONIONS BOILED IN VINEGAR.

⑧ SKILLYGOLEE— OATMEAL BROTH MIXED WITH SALT WATER AND ADDED TO BOILED BEEF.

⑨ IF YOU RUN OUT OF FOOD YOU CAN EAT THE RATS. CLEM SAYS AN OLD SAILOR CALLED ED TARRE IS FEEDING THE RATS CRUMBS TO FATTEN THEM UP—JUST IN CASE!

It turned out that these were the good things about a sea voyage. Clem moved on to the nasty things.

HE TOLD ME ABOUT SCURVY. IT'S A DISEASE YOU GET ABOARD SHIP WHEN YOU DON'T GET ENOUGH FRESH FRUIT AND VEG.

YOU GET SUNKEN EYES

YOU SUFFER 'SLEEPINESS'

YOUR TEETH FALL OUT

YOU DROP DEAD

HE TOLD ME ABOUT THE PUNISHMENTS YOU GET IF YOU MISBEHAVE

LASHED WITH THE CAT-O'-NINE-TAILS

CHAINED TO THE BILBOES IN THE DARKEST, DEEPEST, SMELLIEST PART OF THE SHIP.

THE BILGES – STINKING AND DAMP

← THE BILBOES

I was glad to get off that ship! I wished Clem luck and hurried on my way.

When I got home, Sir Sydney wasn't there but the Countess was. She was furious.

I kept my mouth shut about the errands I had been doing. Then the Countess sent *me* to the Tower!

The Tower of London is a pretty scary place.

I WAS TO REPORT TO
THE LION GATE ①. THERE'S A HUGE
MOAT ② THAT GOES ROUND
THE TOWER. I MET THE OLD
MAN FROM THE BRIDGE AGAIN.
HE SAID THAT PEOPLE WHO
GO INTO THE TOWER DON'T OFTEN
COME OUT AGAIN (THANKS!).
HE SAID PRISONERS WERE
OFTEN KEPT IN THE SALT
TOWER ③. THEN THEY WERE
TAKEN THROUGH AN
UNDERGROUND PASSAGE
TO BE TORTURED IN THE
GREAT WHITE TOWER ④.
HE SAID THE QUEEN'S
MOTHER GOT THE CHOP
IN THE TOWER AND I WAS
TO LOOK OUT FOR HER GHOST
WHICH WALKS NEAR THE
CHURCH ⑤ OR THE EXECUTION
SPOT ⑥. HE REALLY
CHEERED ME UP.

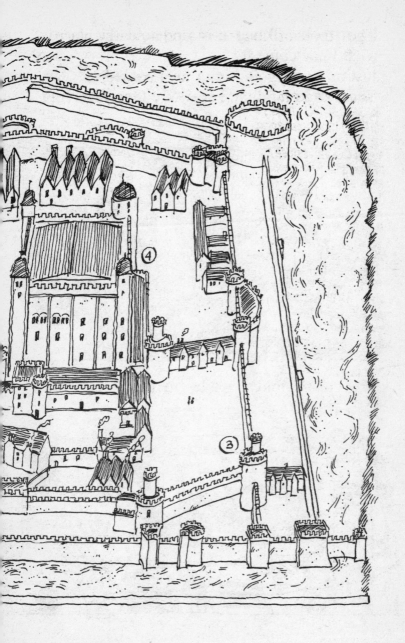

I got to the Tower gate and told the guards what I had come for.

Just as I was going in, a man passed me. His face looked familiar. I was sure I had seen him before.

The guards told a gaoler to take me to Sir Sydney.

We went through a gate then we stopped at another gate. It was a water-gate where prisoners are brought into the Tower by boat on the river.

I recognized the prisoners! One was the man I met in Saint Paul's. The other one was the actor.

We went through yet another gate. I caught a glimpse of the torture chamber through a door.

As we crossed the yard, I saw a block of wood.

I saw a man with an axe.

I saw Sir Sydney being escorted across the yard. He laid his head on the block and...

I was just wondering what to do with his supper, when...

Then they all burst out laughing.

I didn't find it funny. It was horrible. Did they know who had delivered Sir Sydney's letters? I wasn't going to hang around to find out. I ran to the river as fast as I could. A voyage with Clem suddenly seemed a really good idea.

Trevor Twynbarrow spent the rest of his life at sea. He became a successful pirate. He claimed he got the impressive scar on his left cheek during a duel. In fact, he got it when his knife slipped while trying to eat a very tough piece of meat. He owned a large collection of piss-pots and was eventually eaten by a shark off the coast of Brazil.